RANCE
ITALY
GREECE
TURKEY
TUNISIA
MEDITERRANEAN SEA
LIBYA
EGYPT
RA

To Naoual and the women weavers of the Association Tifawin
and to Haj Ahmed Ezzarghani and the apprentice storytellers of Café Clock,
for sharing and preserving their culture for the future

Special thanks to Kate LaBore, Susan Davis, Melissa Topacio Long,
Rachida M'Rabet, Mehdi El Ghaly, and Richard Hamilton

atheneum

ATHENEUM BOOKS FOR YOUNG READERS
An imprint of Simon & Schuster Children's Publishing Division
1230 Avenue of the Americas, New York, New York 10020

Book design by Ann Bobco and Evan Turk
The text for this book is set in Centaur MT Std.
The illustrations for this book are rendered in water-soluble crayon, colored drawing pencils, inks, indigo, sugared green tea, a heat gun, and fire.
Manufactured in China
0416 SCP
First Edition
10 9 8 7 6 5 4 3 2 1
Library of Congress Cataloging-in-Publication Data
Turk, Evan, author, illustrator.
The storyteller / Evan Turk. — First edition.
pages cm
Summary: In a time of drought in the Kingdom of Morocco, a storyteller and a boy weave a tale to thwart a djinn and his sandstorm from destroying their city.
ISBN 978-1-4814-3518-5 (hardcover)
ISBN 978-1-4814-3519-2 (eBook)
1. Storytellers—Juvenile fiction. 2. Storytelling—Juvenile fiction. 3. Droughts—Morocco—Juvenile fiction. 4. Djinn—Juvenile fiction. 5. Morocco—Juvenile fiction. [1. Storytelling—Fiction. 2. Droughts—Fiction. 3. Genies—Fiction. 4. Morocco—Fiction.] I. Title.
PZ7.1.T874St 2016
[E]—dc23
2014044090

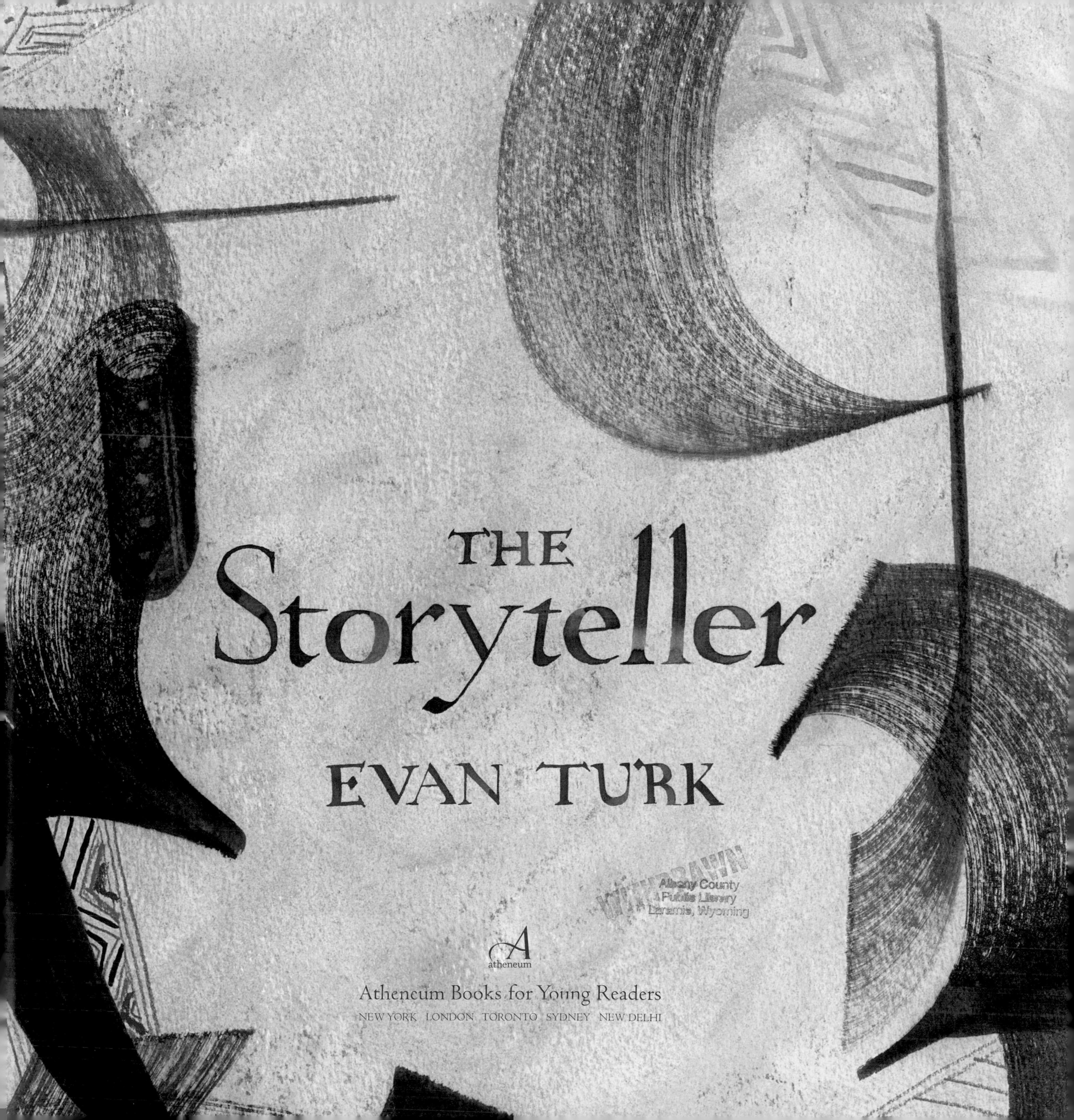

THE Storyteller

EVAN TURK

atheneum

Atheneum Books for Young Readers
NEW YORK LONDON TORONTO SYDNEY NEW DELHI

Long, Long Ago,

like a pearl around a grain of sand, the fertile Kingdom of Morocco formed near the edge of the great, dry Sahara. It had fountains of cool, delicious water to quench the dangerous thirst of the desert, and storytellers to bring the people together.

But as the kingdom grew and life became easier, the people forgot their fear of the desert. Soon they forgot the fountains and the storytellers, too. One by one, the voices of the storytellers were drowned out by noise and silenced by age, and one by one the fountains dried up.

As the last fountain dried, far away in the Sahara a great wind began to stir.

At that same moment, in the hot, dry south of the kingdom, a thirsty young boy made his way through the clamor and smoke of the Great Square to look for a drink, but no one had any water to give.

"Our fountains have run dry," the last water-seller said. "But here, take one of my brass cups. If you find water, you can drink and share it with others."

As the boy walked home, a voice called out to him. “My boy, are you looking for something to drink?”

A withered old man was perched on the edge of a dry fountain.

“That fountain doesn’t have any water!” the boy said.

The man’s face cracked like dry mud to reveal a toothless grin. “Sit down, my boy, and your thirst shall be quenched.”

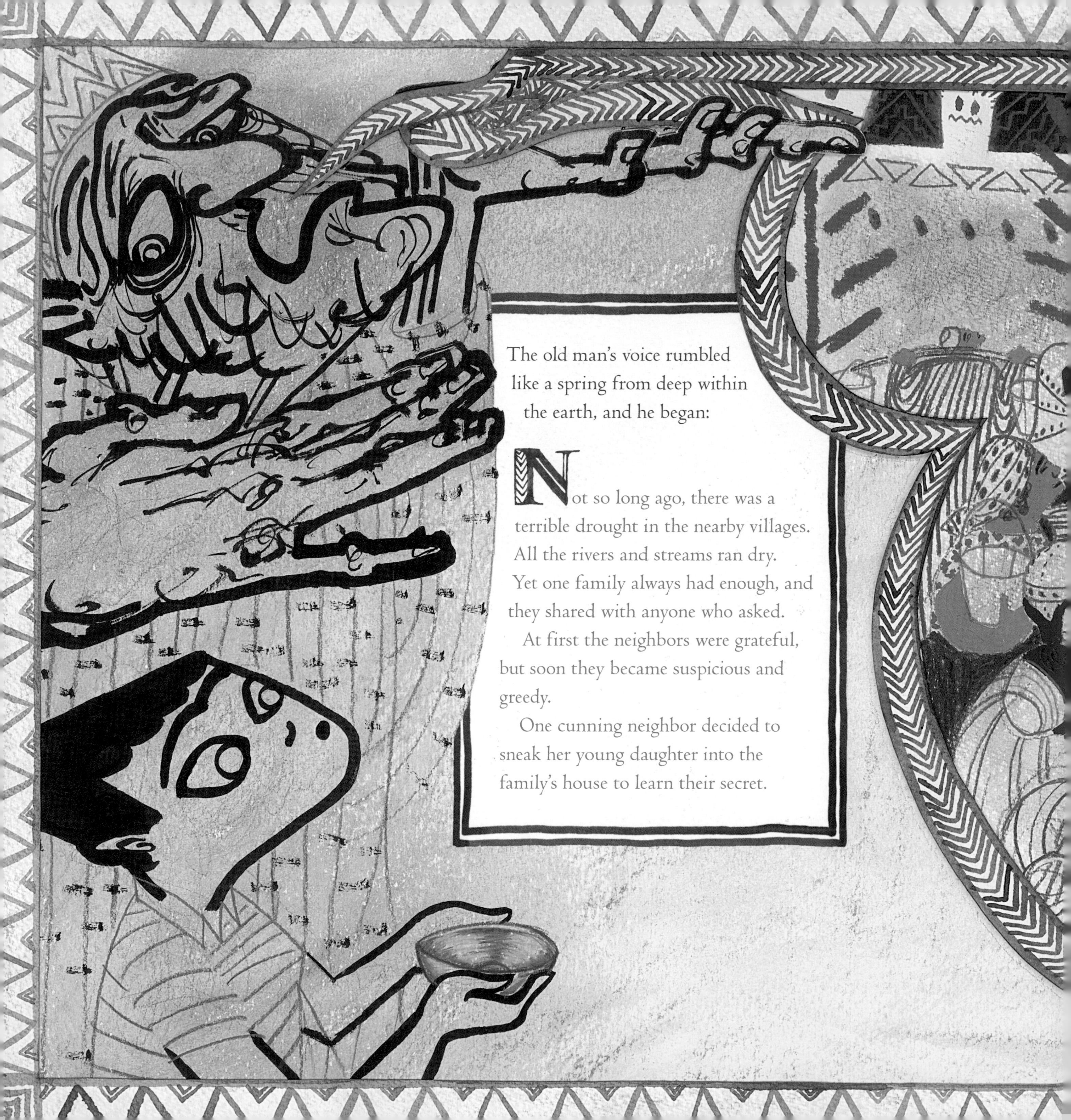

The old man's voice rumbled like a spring from deep within the earth, and he began:

Not so long ago, there was a terrible drought in the nearby villages. All the rivers and streams ran dry.

Yet one family always had enough, and they shared with anyone who asked.

At first the neighbors were grateful, but soon they became suspicious and greedy.

One cunning neighbor decided to sneak her young daughter into the family's house to learn their secret.

There she met a blind woman.

Pretending to be the woman's granddaughter, she asked in her sweetest voice, "Won't you please tell me why we always have water?"

The blind woman laughed a gravelly laugh. "Our family has never been in want of water, thanks to the great blue bird that lives in our courtyard. I was given the bird by my mother, and she by hers, and so on, back a thousand years. And for a thousand years, the glittering bird has always flown and found us water, no matter how dry the land becomes."

"But where did the bird come from?"

The blind woman smiled and replied, "Ah, well, that is a story for another day."

As the old man uttered these words, the boy discovered that his brass cup was full of cool water.

He gasped and looked up at the storyteller. "But what about the bird?" he asked.

"Come back tomorrow, and I shall tell you the story of the Glorious Blue Water Bird."

The boy gulped down his water and rushed home.

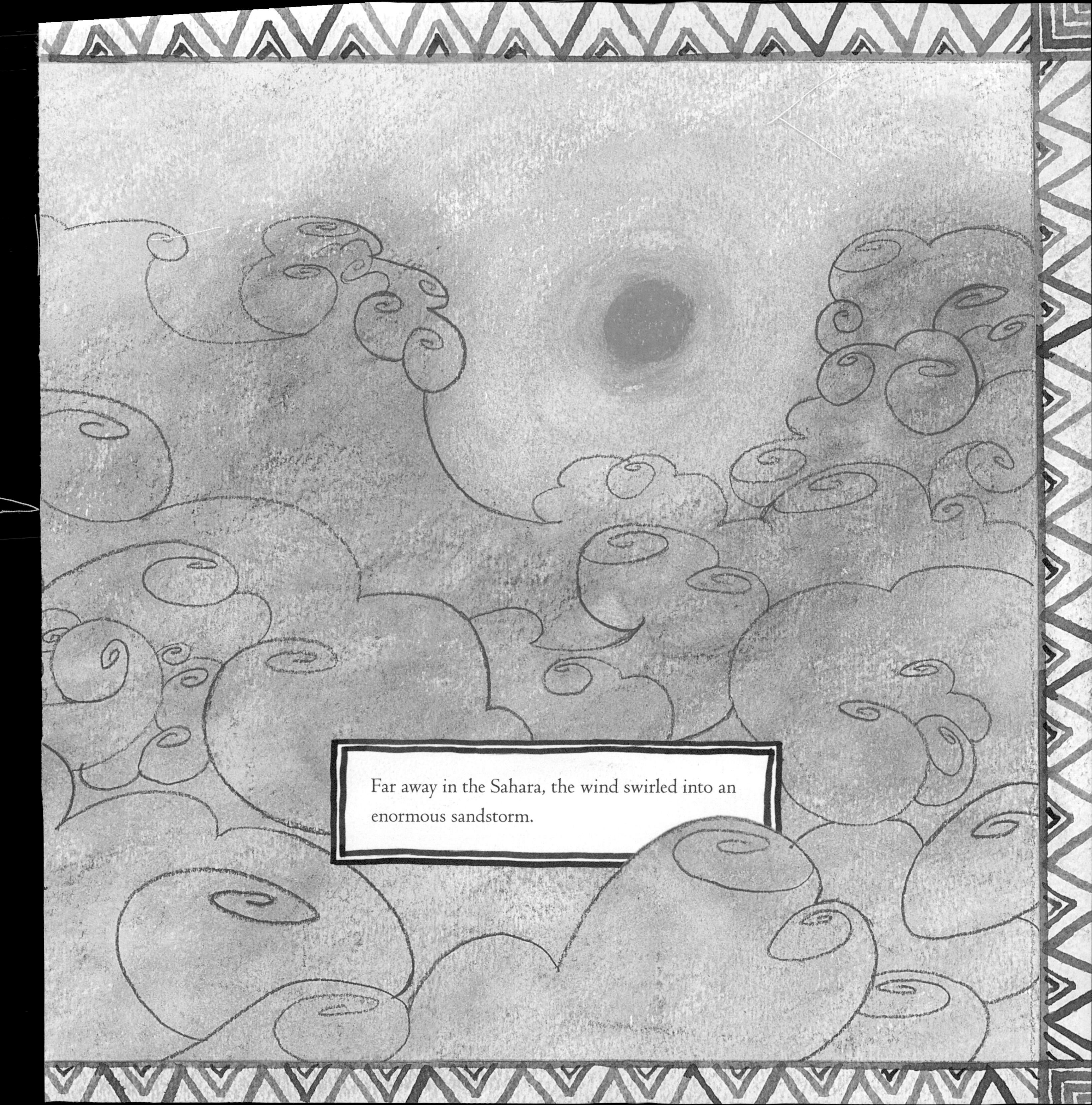
Far away in the Sahara, the wind swirled into an enormous sandstorm.

The next morning, the boy awoke at dawn and ran to meet the storyteller at the fountain again.

"Would you like to hear the story of the Glorious Blue Water Bird?" he asked.

The boy nodded, and the old man began:

"The next day, the little girl snuck in and asked the blind woman again, 'Where did the bird come from?'

Ah, yes. Many years ago, my great-great-grandmother's great-great-grandmother was a carpet weaver. Our village again had a terrible drought, and people had to travel far to find water.

One day, a very old woman walked into the weaver's home with a bundle wrapped in cloth.

"My dear, are you thirsty?" she asked.

"Oh my, yes!" the weaver replied. "We haven't a drop in our whole village!"

The old woman smiled and unwrapped her bundle to reveal a spindle of the most beautiful shimmering blue yarn.

"I was once a weaver as well," she said, "but I have grown old and can no longer trust my hands. Please take this yarn and create something for the people to hope for, and I promise your thirst will be quenched."

"Where did you come by this beautiful yarn?"

The old woman chuckled and replied, "Ah, well, that is a story for another day." And she left.

The old man smiled, and again, the boy's brass cup was full of beautiful, clear water.

"But what about the yarn?" the boy asked.

"Come back tomorrow, and I shall tell you the story of the Miraculous Yarn."

So the boy drank his water and headed home.

Not so far away in the Sahara, the sandstorm gathered and grew and blocked out the sun.

The boy came back the next day, eager to hear the rest of the story.

The storyteller cleared his throat, and his voice poured out:

"The next day, the old woman returned to the weaver's home to find her struggling with the yarn.

"'I don't know how to begin!' the weaver said. 'It is as if my mind unravels in front of the loom.'

"'Ah, yes,' said the old woman, 'You must first find hope for yourself before you can weave it for others. Let me tell you the story of this Miraculous Yarn:

When I was young and beautiful, I was a princess, and I was to marry a prince. I did not love him, and so the night before my wedding, I escaped into the desert with only a camel and my life.

I wandered across the dunes for so long that I could no longer count the days.

I thought myself near death until there appeared what I thought must surely be a mirage.

There in a deep valley was a loom and an enormous pile of yarn of every color.

I collapsed in the sand and wept in despair. Yet as I stared at the yarn, I noticed a blue glimmer, and I began to hope. I picked up the end of the sparkling yarn you see before you and began to weave it into a carpet of shimmering blue.

Within hours I had woven the finest carpet in the land. I laid it out into the center of the valley and fell asleep.

When I awoke, the carpet had turned into a beautiful clear pool, and I drank until I could take no more.

Renewed, I sat in front of the loom and began to weave again: clay red for a house to keep me safe from sand and wind; emerald green for a grove of palm trees to give me shade; bright gold and copper for juicy dates to satisfy my hunger. I kept weaving until I had birthed an entire kingdom.

When I was finished, the only yarn left was this spindle of blue, which never seemed to run out.

With tears in her eyes, the carpet weaver smiled at the old woman. She gathered the women of her family together, and in a flurry they began tying knots, one by one. The yarn came alive in their fingers, and soon a glorious bird awakened and emerged from the loom.

It burst out the door with a buoyant cry and disappeared into the sky.

It returned only moments later carrying buckets full of fresh, clear water, which it poured into the well.

Again and again it flew until the well overflowed and the village was saved.

The little girl thanked the blind woman for her story. Then she crept out the door to tell her mother, who hatched a plan to steal the bird.

Late that night, the mother snuck into the neighbors' courtyard. There, she spied the most beautiful creature she had ever seen, glittering like a sapphire in the moonlight. She fell to her knees and wept.

The family came out into the courtyard to find their neighbor on the floor. "Good neighbor, why do you weep? And why are you in our home?"

"In greed, I came to steal this bird. But, once in its presence, I was filled with hope instead. Reflected in its feathers, I saw myself."

The family brought her inside, and they shared a pot of sweet tea with fresh mint as she dried her eyes. No one ever tried to steal the bird again, and the village never again went without water.

With this, the old man finished, and the boy's brass cup overflowed with water. The boy sipped from it and poured the rest into the fountain.

At that very moment, the sandstorm arrived at the gate to the city in the form of an enormous djinn.

His voice boomed across the trembling walls. "I am the desert, and now that your fountains are gone, I shall destroy your city at sundown and make you part of the desert again."

The boy and the storyteller smiled at each other, and the boy ran to the gate.

"Oh mighty Sahara, before you destroy us, let me tell you a tale and perhaps you will reconsider!" he shouted into the wind.

"I have made up my mind, but you may continue, and then I will destroy your city at sundown."

And so the boy began to tell the tale of the Endless Drought. The djinn was intrigued and failed to notice the sun setting.

"But what about the bird?" he asked when the boy had finished. It was nearly dark now, and a small circle of people had formed.

"Ah, well, that is a story for another day," the boy replied. "If you spare our city tonight, tomorrow I will tell you the tale of the Glorious Blue Water Bird."

The djinn agreed and faded into the desert for the night.

The next afternoon, the boy brought together all the water-sellers from the square and asked them to give a brass cup to anyone who came to listen.

The djinn arrived at the gate and said, “Tell me your tale, and then I will destroy your city at sundown.”

The boy began the tale. As he did, more and more people crowded around, and each one was given a brass cup. The djinn again failed to notice the sun setting as the boy told his story, and by the end the sun had been down for some time. The crowd gasped to see their cups full of water.

“But what about the yarn?” the djinn asked.

“Ah, well, that is a story for another day,” the boy said. “If you spare our city tonight, tomorrow I will tell you the story of the Miraculous Yarn.”

The djinn yawned, agreed, and disappeared back into the desert. The boy then had everyone pour their water into the fountains.

The next day, the entire city circled around the boy to hear his tale, and soon the djinn arrived as well.

"Tell me your tale, and then I will destroy your city at sundown."

The boy began. As his voice rose, the Great Square fell silent. The audience began pouring their cups of water into the fountains, and by the end of the tale the fountains were gurgling again.

The djinn was so entranced that he didn't notice any of this.

"What clever stories, my boy, but, alas, now I must destroy your city."

But when the sandstorm began to push against the walls, water began to gush from every fountain. The djinn found himself hopelessly overpowered.

With one final roar from the crowd, the djinn fell back in defeat. At last, he retreated farther and farther until he was deep in the dunes of the Sahara. . . .

"... And that," said the storyteller, "is the story of how, not long ago, a young boy saved Morocco from the desert."

"But what happened to the boy?" asked a small girl in the audience.

"Ah, well," he replied with a wink,
"that is a story for another day."

AUTHOR'S NOTE

When a storyteller dies, a library burns.
—old Moroccan saying

There is a unique kind of magic that comes from hearing a story told. With only the power of a voice, an entire world can be created. Suddenly, the audience becomes the hero, the villain, or the magic djinn commanding the desert sandstorm. Most importantly, once the story is over, all you need to share it with others is your own voice.

Morocco's public storytellers, or *hlaykia,* have been learning, preserving, and sharing stories for nearly one thousand years. These stories have been passed down from generation to generation and have become a part of the cultural fabric. The power of these storytellers lies in their audience, or *halka,* meaning "circle," "ring," or "link." With the *hlaykia* in the center, the audience forms an expanding circle and is linked with the generations who came before them through the stories.

But these storytellers are disappearing. As audiences drift toward television, movies, and the Internet, there is no one for the aging *hlaykia* to pass their stories along to. Only a handful of master storytellers remain.

Recently, there has been a resurgence in storytelling at a restaurant called Café Clock in the city of Marrakech, where young Moroccans learn from a master storyteller and take ownership of their culture. Morocco, like countries all over the world, including the United States, is at a crossroads, where the future threatens to eclipse what is beautiful about the past. Traditions like storytelling and carpet weaving are vanishing all over the world. It is up to all of us to realize the magic of these things and share them with others, before they disappear.

Further Learning:

Association Tifawin: Weavers of Anzal (Traditional carpet weaving collective in Morocco)
anzal-weavers.com

Hikayat Morocco—Marrakech: storytelling program with Café Clock
hikayatmorocco.weebly.com
marrakech.cafeclock.com

Hamilton, Richard. *The Last Storytellers: Tales from the Heart of Morocco.* London: I. B. Tauris, 2011.

Tales from the Thousand and One Nights. Translated by N. J. Dawood, 1954, 1955, 1957. Reprint, London: Penguin Group, 1973.